THE CASE OF THE MISSING TEEN

A Sera Craven Mystery

KATHLEEN GUIRE

Chapter 1

Isabella arrived on Christmas with all her belongings in a black trash bag. My sister Isabella became part of the Craven family soon after I did. Finding her was the most important mystery I had ever solved.

Isabella tossed a bathing suit in her floral suitcase, the one mom had given her.

My obsession with Nancy Drew began when I was an orphan. In the Colombian orphanage, I had lugged around three donated copies. Ever since I discovered the girl sleuth, I have been reading, rereading, and solving mysteries. I smoothed my plaid capris, feeling the soft fabric as I slipped on my penny loafers.

Nancy Drew said, "You have to wear pants and penny loafers to sleuth." I was excited to practice some sleuthing on our family vacation. My Kindle landed with a soft thud in my backpack, nestled amongst my other essentials. It was a relief to see my digital collection of Nancy Drew books stored on my e-reader, eliminating the need to haul around heavy hardcover copies.

"Mandy's on her way," Mom called up the stairs.

My friend Mandy was joining us on our vacation on the Isle of Tropics Beach. I couldn't call her my best friend anymore because of Isabella. When I made the mistake of calling Mandy my best friend after Isabella joined the family, it didn't go so well. Isabella cried and screamed and hid under the bed for two hours. I overheard Mom on a Zoom call with a therapist mention the words "Reactive Attachment Disorder."

To avoid triggering her attachment disorder, I refrained from calling Mandy or anyone my "best friend." I never expected that my search for her would lead me to a fractured version of who she once was. I could fix her, right?

According to the schedule on the whiteboard, we were supposed to be taking our suitcases down to the front door. Isabella had packed exactly one thing. Her bathing suit. I had packed my suitcase with gallon baggies labeled with Monday, Tuesday, and every day of the trip. I'd organized my outfits, so I didn't waste any beach or mystery-solving time.

"Let's get you packed, Isabella," I said as if I were speaking to a toddler instead of a tween. "Here," I shoved a gallon baggy at her. "Put an outfit in here."

Fifteen minutes later, with me doing most of the work, we packed Isabella's suitcase. She'd half-heart-edly thrown shorts and tanks at me.

"I don't want to go," Isabella said, stomping her foot. Her black curls nodded in agreement. I zipped up her floral suitcase and handed her the handle.

"Maybe we will discover a mystery to solve," I encouraged.

The Craven family had traveled exactly nowhere for the past six months while "we jumped through hoops" - dad's explanation.

"Just a formality," the social worker, Melanie had said, referring to the hoops- visits, therapists, and trauma training for mom and dad.

With her adoption now final, we were free to travel outside the state.

I climbed into the brand-new Toyota van and breathed in the fresh leather. Mom and Dad had shared they imagined the family enjoying road trip snacks and drinks in the comfortable, roomy seats. I hoped this trip would fulfill their joy-filled-family-vision. The Craven family had expanded from two children, Sam and Josiah, to four, and five, if you included Mandy. With Mandy in our group, there were no empty seats.

Dad repacked the trunk while giving Josiah packing pointers while we waited for Mom and Mandy.

"I forgot to fill my water bottle," Isabella moaned.

I returned inside to fill a water bottle for Isabella. In a last-minute rush, Mom scurried around the kitchen, double-checking her list and wiping the counters.

Mandy's dad pulled up in his forest green Subaru,

and Mandy hopped out of the car. Isabella and I both ran to greet her. Three sleuths, that's what we were, ready for a mystery-filled vacation. Sam sometimes joined us in sleuthing when he wasn't in one of his "that's stupid" moods. Josiah just listened to our adventure stories and ruffled our hair and grinned. This family thing was working out pretty well.

It took a while, but now we're all buckled up. Mom ran in one last time to check something.

Dad observed, "We're moving out like a herd of turtles."

I usually asked when I didn't understand a phrase. This time I didn't. I only wished to get this vacation underway and dad's explanations could drag on for fifteen minutes including word origins and Greek and Latin roots. Five minutes later, we merged onto the interstate.

"Which Nancy Drew book do you want to listen to Isabella?"

I had learned to let Isabella and Mandy take turns choosing because they argued about stuff like that. Mom said Mandy was jealous of Isabella. I didn't know why. They were both important to me. Sometimes when they argued, I felt like the melted cheese in a quesadilla. I wanted to slide off the plate like the hot cheese did. Mom said I made a good peacemaker because I was a good sleuth.

"You're good at detecting people's feelings, Sera. Just be careful you don't ignore your own," she said one day after Mandy had left. Isabella and Mandy had argued about everything that day. I was dizzy from looking back and forth between them and trying to keep the peace. After an exhausting day, Mom wasn't sure Mandy should come on vacation with us. Isabella and I had begged, and Mom had relented. I hoped they would remember how hard we fought to include Mandy and agree on the book.

"*The Hidden Staircase*," Mandy said, not giving Isabella the chance to cast the first vote.

"No," Isabella shot back. "You always pick. I want to choose."

"What do you want to listen to?" I asked, trying to maintain the peace. We hadn't even been in the van for an hour and a fight was brewing. Despite my dad setting the air conditioning to sixty-five, beads of sweat danced on my forehead. I wiped them away and smiled, swallowing my anxiety.

"I don't know," Isabella said. "Whatever she doesn't want to listen to."

Mom must have seen my distress in the rearview mirror. "How about Mom chooses?" she said.

Isabella crossed her arms and rocked back and forth in the leather seat as if it were a rocking chair.

"Okay," she huffed. "I'm not listening."

Mom chose *The Hidden Staircase*.

I brought a headphone jack splitter so we could all listen without bothering others in the van. Isabella maintained her I'm-not-listening-stance. I pressed the play button on the Kindle and gazed out the window, reminiscing about the past six months, the quality time we spent as a family, and all the mysteries we, sometimes four of us, had unraveled. The best mystery had started with a lost watch at the outlets and led us to finding Isabella. I hung onto that thought. Finding Isabella was one of the best days of my life. When we were orphans together, I promised I'd find her when we were separated. She'd been adopted and brought to the United States. After joining the Craven family, I set out to find her. I did it. I just didn't know the ones following finding her would be so difficult.

Most of our mysteries had been minor ones-when Mom lost her favorite pen, or the time her credit card slid down under the driver's side seat after she paid at Starbucks. She couldn't find it for two days. There was the time Sam lost his book report. It turned out that he hadn't written it. He asked me "to keep her off my back." To avoid Mom's nagging for a while, he used the services of the "three sleuths," which had me cracking up. I tried to picture Mom hopping on his back and I laughed out loud. Sam just got super mad and made fun of my plaid pants. He threatened not to pay us the five-dollar fee. Dad stepped in and made him pay *and* write the report.

Isabella poked me. "Do you think we will find a good mystery to solve at the beach?"

I guess I wasn't the only one thinking about mysteries. I pushed the pause button on the book so we could talk.

"I hope so," I said.

"Do you think we will find a dead body?" Mandy asked. She shivered and wrung her hands.

"If you do, count me in," Sam said.

"You're not going to find a dead body," Josiah said, as he laughed.

"If you find a dead body, we are going home," Mom said.

"Okay, maybe not a dead body. What other kinds of mystery can we solve?" I asked.

"Maybe find a buried treasure?" Sam said. "A treasure would be cool."

"It would be, but don't we need a map for one of those?" I asked.

"That's true," Isabella said. "Does anyone have one of those?"

"I've run out of treasure maps," Dad said, and we couldn't help but laugh.

I knew we'd discover a puzzle to unravel when we reached the beach. My bones sensed it, just like Grandpa's knees and the approaching bad weather.

We ended up playing roadside alphabet and then joined Sam and Josiah for a movie called "The Court Jester." Isabella and Mandy acted as if they'd forgotten the tiff earlier. The movie maintained the peace for a few hours.

The movie ended and tension in the air was palpable as the scent of frustration and anger wafted through the van. Mandy and Isabella quarreled about seating arrangements, which book to listen to, and who knew me better. Why had I asked Mandy to come? For the briefest of moments, I wish Isabella had stayed home. Not Mandy.

Isabella wriggled out of her seatbelt and crawled towards the plush captain chairs where Sam and Josiah sat.

"Change seats with me Sam, I can't sit with those two mentally arranged people anymore."

"You mean deranged?" Sam playfully prodded her shoulder with his sleek iPad, provoking a swift reaction as she swatted it from his grasp. He unbuckled and reached down to pick it up. Before he could grab it, Isabella got there first and rolled down the window.

"I'm rearranging your Ipad," she yelled over the howl of the wind, whistling through the van and whipping her hair into a frizzy frenzy and sucking the air out of my lungs, which crumpled like tortilla chips at the bottom of a bowl.

"What the cuss?" Sam said, except he said the other word that would land him in t-r-o-u-b-l-e.

"Samuel," Dad warned, using his full name, which meant there would be a consequence.

Josiah reached out, his hand snatching the iPad from danger before rolling up the window. Isabella's body slumped onto the floor as she swayed gently, seeking solace in the rhythmic movement.

"You're going to punish me?" Sam asked. She was dangling my tablet out the window. She never gets in trouble." He slammed the Ipad case cover shut after giving it a thorough once over and then stuffed it in the holder behind the passenger seat mom was sitting in.

I held my breath. As much as I hated to admit it. Sam was right. This time. Isabella rarely got in trouble, and when she did, our parents quickly let her off the hook.

Dad let out a heavy sigh and tightened his grip on the steering wheel. The tension was thicker than refried beans on a cold taco.

"Isabella, you need to apologize to Sam."

"No," she said, rocking back and forth faster. "He hates me. He doesn't deserve to have an Ipad."

"I think it's time for a rest break," Mom said.

Dad jerked the vehicle over to the exit lane, hitting rumble strips that jarred the vehicle in syncopated rhythm, mirroring the emotional jarring Isabella was creating in the vehicle.

Once we parked and unfolded ourselves from the seats, Sam stalked off to the men's room. Isabella smiled. If I didn't know any better, I'd say she was a villain from one of Nancy Drew's mysteries.

As we strolled around the rest area, the cool breeze brushed against our skin, refreshing us after a long drive.

Dad suggested we "stretch our legs."

No one did any stretching. The English language is odd. I still had to ask what phrases meant. Mandy helped me a lot. Isabella struggled more than I did, which was strange because she had been in the country longer. She had been adopted by an American family before me. Because of several failed adoptions, she experienced being shuffled from family to family. Maybe the trauma of shifting from family to family slowed her learning. It was amusing to hear her jumble up expressions. I tried not to laugh. I also tried to help her. Helping her is a gamble because she is stubborn. She frequently stumbles over incorrect phrases, unwilling to acknowledge her mistakes.

After Mom pulled a cooler out of the back, we all grabbed a few things and made our way to a picnic table Dad had claimed.

"I have the table clothes," Isabella declared, the fabric rustling as she waved it in the air.

"Table cloth," Sam said in a growl.

"Is it clothes for the table?" she asked.

"Yes," Mom said. She shot Sam a warning look.

It was too late. Sam was on a roll.

"We have Nancy Drew, Barbie, and Yogi Berra."

"And I have the flagon with the dragon," Josiah added. He had a talent for creating a positive and cheerful environment.

"Is it the brew that is true?" I asked.

With a swift motion, Josiah swung the water bottles onto the table.

"The chalice with the palace has the pellet with the poison," Dad joined in, quoting the famous line from "The Court Jester."

We three girls danced around the table reciting the rhymes from the Court Jester until we were breathless. We attempted to drown out Sam's comment, replacing it with the comforting sounds of laughter and conversation. As I watched, Isabella twirled and smiled.

She has come far since joining the family. At the beginning, she had raging fits. She lied. Stole things from every member of the family and ruined every family event. Mom called it survival mode. She told me Isabella needed to feel safe and trust us before she could let those behaviors go. I had my coping mechanism; she said -solving mysteries. Mom's knowledge of this matter stemmed from her time in a group home during her youth.

When Sam made fun of my detective outfits, I felt somehow wrong for being me. Like I didn't deserve to be part of a family or even exist. I was tempted to stop sleuthing to fit in, but the thought of life without a mystery to solve felt empty. I didn't want Isabella to feel that way. I wanted her to feel wanted. I didn't want him to say those things.

"Okay, girls, calm down and sit down," Mom said.

Mom unpacked lunch and handed out sandwiches and chips. I could almost taste the combination of flavors - the soft bread, the tangy mayo, and the salty crunch of the chips. I didn't even have the chance to take my first bite when a curly-haired dog appeared and ran under the table.

As if on cue, Mandy, Isabella, and I dropped our heads, resembling puppets on a string.

"Rusty!" a woman's voice yelled.

"Darn, I thought we had a mystery," Mandy said, referring to the lost dog and shaking her blonde head.

A woman wearing bright pink lipstick and white

blonde curls jogged up to the picnic table. Standing in between my sister and me, she made us look like an oreo, with her fair skin contrasting with our dark skin.

"I'm so sorry, he got away from me," she crouched down and put her head under the table. Rusty crunched a chip that had fallen on the ground. After glancing at the pink-lipstick girl, he continued eating.

'Rusty, come out now," she said, stomping her foot. She turned her attention to us and smiled. "Hi, my name is Lemon."

"Like the fruit?" Isabella asked. She laughed. Sam joined her.

"Kids, don't be rude," Dad said. Sam and Isabella were getting along in all the wrong areas.

Mom took over and introduced us all. After finishing his chip, Rusty slinked out from under the table. Lemon snapped a leash on him.

"I was taking a picture and he bolted," Lemon held up her camera as proof.

I decided right then and there that Lemon understood sleuthing for two reasons. She sported pink plaid clam diggers and was in possession of a camera.

"We are going to the beach for vacation, The Isle of Tropics" I mentioned, imagining the warm sun on my skin and the cool touch of wet sand between my toes. "I like your pants."

"Thank you. I'm headed to the Isle of Tropics too. I'm going to photograph my cousin's wedding and take a little vacation too."

"Are you a wedding photographer?" Mom asked.

"Nope. Forensic Photographer for the FBI."

"Nice meeting you all, have a great trip."

"Pleasure to meet you," Dad and Mom said simultaneously.

Rusty tugged the leash, Lemon followed, her words trailing off and drowned out by a semi truck's brakes releasing air like a giant whoopee cushion.

We needed a real mystery to solve. Perhaps if we arrive at the beach, we might find one if we hung around a certain Forensic Photographer named Lemon.

Chapter 2

A giant ball of pink sun sank into the ocean when we arrived. All of us ran down to the beach to soak it all in before we unloaded the car. Sam, Isabella, Mandy, and I didn't stop running until the water sloshed over our knees and soaked our shorts. The frothy waves sucked us in. With the sun down, the beach floor darkened. Tiny lights appeared and zipped across the sand.

"What are those?" I yelled.

"Those are ghost crabs," Josiah yelled back. "Come see."

A ghost crab scuttled sideways across the sand, snapping his pincers. He froze when I caught him in my sight.

Isabella and Sam stayed in the water. Mandy and I zigged and zagged, chasing the glowing crabs and laughing. Mom grabbed her phone and snapped a few pictures. I turned and ran into the darkness again. I hit something hard and tumbled backward.

"I'm sorry," a voice said.

"Lemon?" Mom said.

"Yes?"

"We met at the rest area," Mom explained.

"Oh, yes, the Craven family."

"Is the wedding here?" I asked, righting myself and finding my footing.

"Yes, here at Isle of Tropics."

"Where is the church?" I asked, looking around.

"Oh," Lemon laughed. "The wedding is on the beach."

"That's nice," Mom said.

"Right now, I'm trying to get some photos of these ghost crabs. You kids want to help?"

Magically, Sam and Isabella appeared. This kind of help was right up their alley. We all spent the next fifteen minutes herding ghost crabs toward Lemon. Such funny little creatures. They dodged. We dodged. We could feel the fine grains of sand slipping through our fingers as we struggled to regain our balance. Lemon laughed so hard she fell on her butt.

Rusty added to the chaos by barking. He nipped at our shorts as we ran by.

"It's time to go in and get cleaned up," Mom said while we were all down on the sand.

"And get the stuff out of the car," Dad said.

I uttered a loud groan when Dad finished his sentence. I didn't feel too bad about it because everyone did except Mom.

"I'm sure I'll see you around," Lemon said as she grabbed Rusty's leash and waved.

We were just carrying the last items, our back-packs. I knew they were our last items because when Sam had grabbed his backpack first, Dad had said, "That's your last item, not your first. Help your Mother."

Mom was holding the door open for me when a woman's voice called from the darkness, "Yoohoo. Hello!"

She stepped into the glow of the porch light.

"Hi, I'm your neighbor Phyllis." She stuck out a hand. Mom didn't offer hers. I think she was too tired to shake hands.

Phyllis must have caught on because she said, "You all must be exhausted. I'm sure we will see you tomorrow on the beach. You can meet the whole family then. I just wanted to warn you we've had some break-ins up and down the beach. She waved her pale arm in an arc.

"Yipee," Sam whispered in my ear. The sharp sound of the smack echoed in the air as Mandy's hand made contact with my arm and backpack. Isabella plowed into Sam and we had a gridlock at the back door.

"It's nothing to be excited about children," Phyllis reprimanded.

"Oh, no. We are sleuths, like Nancy Drew," I explained.

"I loved Nancy Drew when I was a girl." She smiled, showing perfect white teeth. "I kept a list of bad guy traits." Her eyes twinkled.

"I have one of those too," I said.

"We must get inside," Mom said. "Thank you for the warning, Phyllis. I'm sure we will see you tomorrow."

Phyllis turned to leave and we four kids squealed. Josiah groaned.

Mom pushed the four of us kids inside and shut the door, and clicked the keypad to make sure it was locked.

"I knew we would find a mystery to solve!" I yelled.

"And we just got here," Mandy added. We had moved to the girls' bedroom. Isabella claimed the top bunk and had already set up camp there. Mandy and I each got a twin. Sam had taken residence on one. Mandy and I lounged on the other.

"Maybe we should sneak out tonight," Sam said. So, he was on board this time. Good. The only problem was he could get out of hand sometimes. I didn't want us to get in trouble our first night here and be banned from solving mysteries for the entire trip.

"Let's wait until tomorrow," Isabella said. "Those ghost craps freak me out."

"I think you mean crabs," Josiah said, playfully tousling her hair with a mischievous grin. Josiah must have slipped in while we were talking. I'm glad we had decided against Sam's plan or Josiah would have intervened like he did when I was trying to find Isabella.

Sam and Josiah had a room across the hall from

ours. Each bedroom had its own nice bathroom. No fighting over the bathroom with the boys.

The girls' room was painted pink. The bunk beds were white with hot pink comforters. The paintings on the wall were all beach-themed. Starfish and shells. It felt beached. I think mom would say that. And she would like the white. Mom and Dad had the entire third floor to themselves. It was one enormous master suite.

Mom yelled up the stairwell, "Dad is making popcorn, come down!"

Our sleuthing would have to wait. There wasn't anything we could solve tonight. We didn't have any clues. Besides, I was hungry.

Tomorrow, we look for clues," I said as I ran down the stairs.

"Josiah, will you help? Please?"

"Maybe squirt."

"Oh you have to," Mandy added. "We won't be allowed to look for clues ourselves."

"But if you come, we can go anywhere." Mandy begged.

Josiah sighed, "Oh, all right."

This was going to be the best vacation ever. WE had only just arrived and we had a mystery to solve. And even better than a mystery, a whole family to solve it with.

I went to bed that night full of buttery popcorn and happy. In the dim moonlight, Isabella's figure silently slipped into the bed beside me. A few minutes later, Mandy joined us. We whispered and giggled until Josiah stuck his head in the doorway and threatened to get Dad.

———

THE NEXT MORNING AT BREAKFAST, I asked if we kids could take a walk along the beach. Then I jabbed Josiah in the ribs with my elbow.

"I can go with them, Mom and Dad," he offered. I could tell he was reluctant because his shoulders slumped. That's always a clue the person doesn't really want to do what you asked.

"I think that sounds okay," Dad said. "Let's just set a time limit on it, shall we?" Then he winked at me. He knew exactly what we were up to. We had a time limit of one hour before we had to check in. An hour is plenty of time to do some sleuthing.

"What clues should we be looking for?" Isabella said as we jogged down the boardwalk. "Someone auspicious?"

"You mean suspicious," Sam said, playfully knocking into her with his shoulder, causing her to stumble. She lost her balance and fell into the sand.

"Come on you two, this is serious." Josiah pulled Isabella up and helped her dust off. Isabella shook a fist at Sam. I hoped my idea would help her forget the incident.

"I see the first person we can interview." Straight ahead of us was Phyllis. I made a beeline for her. That means I went straight for her. I wasn't sure what that had to do with a bee, but that's what Dad said when we needed to go straight to bed at night.

Phyllis turned and saw us. Mandy waved her notebook in the air, ready to write clues.

"And here are our sleuths," Phyllis said with a smile. I'm not sure who she was saying it to because she was alone.

"COULD WE ASK YOU A FEW QUESTIONS?" I said. We four kids crowded around her in a semicircle. Josiah stood off to the side, kicking sand and looking bored. How could he look bored when we had a mystery to solve? It was so exciting.

"Of course," she said.

"How many houses were robbed?" Mandy asked, reading from her notebook.

"Well, I don't know, exactly," she said, tapping her chin with a finger. Her slender hand had sea blue fingernails with tiny red stars painted on them. "Maybe five or more."

"Have you seen anyone auspicious?" Isabella added in a serious tone.

I didn't have the heart to correct her. She was standing so straight and proud.

Thankfully, Sam didn't either. But that may have been because of the poke in the back Josiah gave him.

"No, I haven't," she said.

"Do the robberies happen at night?" I asked.

. . .

"YOU KNOW. The interesting thing about the robberies is they all happen in the middle of the day," Phyllis put her hands on her waist like Wonder Woman and looked up towards the sky.

"SO... it seems as if the thief knows when people are going to be out," Josiah offered.

"HMMM. YES, THAT'S A GOOD CLUE!" Sam said.

"YES, HE MUST," Phyllis agreed.

"MOM, WE ARE READY TO SWIM!" Two white blond-headed boys ran toward her, sand flying behind them. A tall, lean, fair-skinned man wearing a large sunhat followed.

"THEY ARE full of waffles and ready to go," he said. His bag thudded against the sand as he eagerly trailed behind the twins, their laughter echoing as they frolicked into the crashing waves.

PHYLLIS TURNED to us and said, "Goodbye!" as she ran down the beach into the water with her family.

We walked further down the beach. As we walked

further down, we noticed no one was on the beach. We only saw one other person. George, a weathered fisherman, focused on his line, his eyes fixed on the water as he patiently waited for a bite.

Josiah said, "Let's head back, guys. It's getting hot."

"I'm thirsty," Sam said.

"I want to swim," he added. "That's why we came to get in the ocean. Not sleuth all day."

I looked at Isabella and Mandy. They weren't saying anything, but I could tell they wanted to.

We all turned to head back when Rusty came racing down the beach towards us. His pink tongue hung out of his mouth and his leash dragged behind him. Lemon followed behind him with a camera bouncing around her neck and wearing lemon-yellow pajamas.

Josiah's agile movements blurred as he reached out, snatching the leash just in time, his hand sinking into the soft grains of sand. Rusty pulled, but he was no match for Josiah. "I have him!" he said, spitting sand out of his mouth at the same time.

"How embarrassing. I was just sitting on the deck drinking coffee and taking a few photos. He took off. I'm not even dressed." She swatted at her pajamas as if she could rub them away.

"IT'S OKAY. No one is out here." I said.

"Except George," Mandy added.

23

"And all he cares about is fish," Sam said, kicking the sand.

I FELT the cool breeze brush against my face as I turned towards the spot where George had stood, rod in hand. He was gone. I guess we bugged him too much with our questions. He probably went somewhere else to fish.

Lemon scolded Rusty, and we turned to go home. There was no one else to question. Sam wanted to swim. Josiah was tired of supervising and wanted a drink. Isabella and Mandy were dragging their feet in the sand in front of me. I guess everyone wanted to do something other than trudging up and down the beach in the hot sand.

Ten minutes later, we were back home, changing into our suits. Mom had packed snacks and water. We grabbed towels, and all went to the beach together. While all of us kids (and Dad) were playing in the surf, Phyllis ran down the beach yelling, "We were robbed!"

Chapter 3

I squealed and clapped my hand over my mouth. It was probably rude to squeal in excitement about someone getting robbed. It meant, however, whoever the burglar was, he had been close by. So near we may have seen him walk up to the row of beach houses.

As I swam back toward the beach, the forceful push and pull of the waves against my body left me gasping for breath, fighting to stay afloat. Once free of the water, I ran through the sand. Each step felt like lifting heavy weights as if my feet were encased in solid blocks of concrete. Sam had already finished drying off. How did he get here so fast? Mandy and Isabella came dripping after us.

"Are we going to interstate her?" Isabella asked, breathless and shivering.

"Phyllis?" I asked.

"You mean interrogate," Sam said, hitting her on the rear. Isabella reeled forward and caught herself with a hand in the sand. She glared at him and raised a fist. He smirked and laughed.

"We should ask her some questions. Let me see if she has time," I said, stepping in between Sam and Isabella.

Phyllis swiftly turned on her heels and sprinted back, the boardwalk and colorful beach houses fading into view. I'm sure she needed to talk to the police.

"I know what you kids are up to," Mom said. "You can talk to her later. For now, enjoy the beach."

We four camped out on our towels and talked about what sort of questions we should ask Phyllis.

What was taken?

Was the house locked?

The heat became unbearable after thirty minutes. With the snacks all gone, we made a collective decision to return to the ocean and ride the waves. I couldn't believe it. We had a genuine mystery to solve. We were on vacation. Life couldn't get any more perfect.

I stood and raced toward the water, not stopping until a wave submerged my head. I emerged from the water, my body dripping and my bathing suit skirt clinging to my skin. Laughing. Sam joined me. The cool, refreshing touch of the water enveloped our bodies as we submerged ourselves in the wave. When we came up, Isabella and Mandy joined us. We four linked arms and dove. Following an hour of running into the waves, we dragged ourselves from the water, completely exhausted and starving. I reclined in the surf, allowing it to wash over my feet and legs while the sun dried my torso.

I turned and noticed Josiah's animated gestures and the person's mocking expression as they conversed behind me. I raised up on my elbow. He sounded upset. He didn't get angry unless something was wrong. Maybe he found the burglar and was confronting him! I rolled over on my belly. Sam, Isabella, and Mandy found toweled off.

"Let's go get food," Sam begged, motioning for me to join them.

The tension in the air was almost palpable as Josiah's words carried a hint of warning. "Those are my sisters, so back off!" His face flushed, and he clenched his fists.

The teen's curled lip and dismissive gaze conveyed his contempt as he swiftly pivoted away. He swaggered off. Was that a villain? I thought about my bad guy list and remembered what Josiah had said. You couldn't always tell from the outside. This guy sported a deep tan, and bleached blonde hair with a bandana tied around his curls. What was his intention for Isabella and me?

"What was that about?" I asked. His reaction created a whole new mystery.

"Nothing for you to worry about, squirt. Let's go get some lunch."

Josiah's strong grip enveloped my hand as he effortlessly lifted me, swinging me over his shoulder. He ran up the beach. My breath escaped in a whoosh with every footfall. My stomach threatened to vomit up its contents. Except there were no contents. So, instead, I laughed a staccato laugh with each jarring step.

———

LATER THAT AFTERNOON, we were finally able to interrogate Phyllis. Mandy and Isabella both wanted to take charge of the questioning. I gave them each a question to ask while I took notes. It's challenging to be both a sibling and a friend. You have to put yourself last and others first. Thankfully, Sam was tired and just wanted to tag along, to pick on Isabella, not to ask questions. I'd planned to intervene if he did.

"Did you see anyone auspicious near your home this morning?" Isabella asked proudly.

SAM OPENED his mouth to reply. I slapped him on the back and he coughed instead. Phyllis ignored the word mix-up and answered.

"No, I didn't."

I wrote that down - no suspects.

"Had you locked your door?" Mandy asked.

"Yes, I think so." She was flustered. Her cheeks turned the shade of lipstick Lemon wears. Bright. Pink.

"What if I didn't?" she said. What if the break-in is all my fault? My wedding ring. Tom's watch."

"The robbery is not your fault. Even if you left

your door open." Sam's eyes widened as he empha-
sized his point, his eyebrows lifting in concern.

Thanks, Sam. You are not helping at all.

We had all the information we were going to get
out of Phyllis right now. So I thanked her. We turned
to leave.

I made my way towards our beach house, only a
few houses apart from Phyllis's. While I strolled, a
great idea popped into my head.

"Who was on the beach this morning?" I asked.

"Just George, the fisherman," Sam said.

"Let's go back and ask him if he saw anything,"
Mandy suggested.

"'Zactly what I was thinking," Isabella said.

We stopped to ask Mom if we could go. Josiah
offered to join us. Weird. But okay.

We had just stepped off the boardwalk when the
sneering teen appeared. He was accompanied by two
other teenagers. These two would, without a doubt,
be on my bad guy list. With hands firmly planted on
their hips, all three of them formed a solid barrier,
blocking our path.

"Hey, guys, go back to the house," Josiah said. His
eyes locked with bandana-guy. Isabella and Mandy
turned and ran. Sam and I stayed.

Chapter 4

Sera Craven Mystery 2

I would not leave Josiah. I wouldn't risk him being taken. "The Case of the Missing Person" incident was a close call that taught me about kidnapping. Plus, some kids in the orphanage would gang up on a younger kid and beat them up. Sometimes they wanted something. Sometimes it was just for fun. I didn't know which these guys wanted. I was determined to stay until I found out.

"THIS ONE'S PRETTY," Bandana-guy said. His gaze traveled the length of my body, taking in every detail. "Bring her to the bonfire tonight."

"I'm not coming to the bonfire, I told you that earlier. And leave my sisters alone." Josiah lunged forward.

Suddenly, he found himself surrounded by a

gaggle of teens. Sam and I found ourselves outside of the circle.

"Just do what we ask. Or something worse will happen to your sisters. We only want to have a little fun with them. Bring the blonde one too."

Sam and I exchanged glances. What did we do? Jump on these guys' backs? Run and get dad? Yell for the people down at the beach?

It was a tense few seconds. I froze in indecision. I couldn't abandon Josiah.

There was a low and angry growl behind me, coming from something or someone.

Out of nowhere, a ball of fur dashed out from the sea grass and landed on the person with the bandana. He tugged on his t-shirt until it tore.

"Hey, get your dog off me."

The click of a shutter on a camera.

"Thanks for letting me take your photos, dudes," Lemon said, stepping out from behind a dune.

Rusty persisted in growling and leaping at a second teenager, baring his teeth.

"Hey, stop it. Get your dog," Bandana-guy said.

"Sure," Lemon offered. "As soon as you agree to leave these kids alone."

Rip. Another tee shirt bites the dust.

"I'm calling the police, witch."

"Go right ahead." Lemon said. "I'm sure we have plenty to tell them."

Josiah had joined Sam and me to watch Rusty's show. All three teens broke loose and took off down the beach.

"Thanks, Lemon," Josiah said. "Those guys are bad news."

"I know. I heard everything. I was behind the sand dunes taking photos." she said. "Good boy, Rusty, good boy," she said, ruffling his fur. She slipped him a treat.

"Let's head to your house, guys. I want to talk to your Mom and Dad."

I was ready to go home. I didn't want to question anyone right now. All I wanted was to hug my mom. And Josiah, which I did.

"Hey, squirt," he said with a nervous laugh. "It's okay. I won't let anyone hurt you."

"Neither will I," Sam added in a shaky voice.

Five minutes later, we were sitting in the family room. I leaned on Mom's shoulder and sipped lemon water. Sam's restless knees bounced up and down as he sat on the plush ottoman, his elbows firmly planted on his knees. Josiah and Lemon sat on the couch with dad. Both looked serious.

"I have a recording I'd like to show you," Lemon said.

"Hey, squirt, why don't you go find Isabella and Mandy?" Josiah asked.

Lemon added, "I don't think you want her to be her for this. Sam either."

"Hey, I…" Sam protested.

"Kids, Isabella and Mandy are up in the master suite watching a movie. Go join them." Dad said.

Sam and I obeyed. It was dad's stern voice, which meant he would not change his mind.

"There are plenty of snacks up there. No need to come down until the movie is over," Mom added.

I tromped up the stairs. The sound of Sam's labored breathing echoed through the stairwell, providing cover for my fake ascent. I hid in the stairwell. I gestured with my finger to my lips, silently signaling Sam to halt his ascent. He froze.

Lemon shared the recorded clip with Mom and Dad.

"THESE TEENS ARE the low men on the totem pole, I would imagine." Lemon was explaining.

"WHAT DO YOU MEAN?" Mom asked.

"GET ready for what I'm about to say. There's a human trafficking ring set up here. Temporarily. I think. I would need to contact my co-workers at the FBI for more information and clarification, if that's okay."

There was silence for at least a minute. Sam was breathing like a deer snorting on my neck. I elbowed his chest, and he fell backward.

"Did you hear that?" he hissed. "FBI."

"You work for the FBI," Dad said. "I thought you were a forensic photographer."

"Oh, I am. I rarely tell people that, especially if they have kids. It freaks them out when they find out I take pictures of crime scenes and dead people." she explained.

"Wow, that's so cool!" Sam said, as his punch made me stumble and fall down three stairs.

"Sera, Sam, we can hear you. Go upstairs." Dad commanded.

We complied. He was serious this time. There would be a serious consequence if we disobeyed. We wouldn't get a second chance. Josiah could fill us in later. Sam and I slowly ascended the stairs and flopped onto the bed with Mandy and Isabella, while popcorn fluttered up and descended like heavy snow.

"You guys," Sam said, "Sera and I found a huge mystery this time. Bigger than robbers. This is FBI big." Sam said as if he had invented the whole scenario.

"What?!" Mandy and Isabella said in stereo.

"Yep," I added. "Lemon works for the FBI and she is going to bring more FBI people here!"

"Wow, we have hit the John pot!" Isabella squealed.

"That's jack-pot," Sam said, smiling. Good. He was not making fun of her or putting her down. Who knew a human trafficking case could make him nicer to his sister?

"What can we do to help?" Isabella asked.

"Nothing," Josiah said from the doorway. "I'm serious, guys. You can't solve this one."

"What's Lemon going to do?" I asked.

"She's going to bring a human trafficking expert here. I believe her name is Kat.

Sam exclaimed, "Wow! This is so exciting!"

"I feel like there is something you haven't told us," I said. Mandy shook her head in agreement.

"I'm going to the bonfire tonight. Undercover," Josiah said. "The task force will be here in a few hours to prepare me."

Sam's jaw dropped. His eyes were as big as clam shells. Josiah picked a piece of popcorn off the comforter and threw it in his mouth with a chuckle.

"You guys, listen, you have to stay out of it this time. This is dangerous! He pivoted and sprinted down the staircase.

I had to be a part of this, no matter what. I planned to attend the bonfire. I was going to meet this "Kat" person. This was the opportunity of a lifetime. I deliberately kept it from Mandy, Sam, Isabella, and especially Mom and Dad.

Chapter 5

Agent Kat Gains, her husband Agent Jim, and four members of her task force had arrived an hour ago. I don't know how Josiah convinced Mom and Dad to let him go undercover. After all, it was Josiah who saved me from being trafficked just six months ago, so they knew the danger of him getting involved.

It may have been the four of the members of the task force who showed up from the FBI. Three of them were college students themselves - Joyce, Jordan, and James. Damica, who was a profiler who dad says looks like she is twelve. Josiah had a quick training session with them in the living room. Of course, after they herded Sam and me upstairs to watch a movie, I stumbled upon an air vent that opened to the room below, granting us the ability to listen in. I heard Damica tell Josiah that all they wanted to do tonight is make contact.

"Just be cool. Don't make a scene. And more

importantly than anything, act like you agree with everything they say. Watch your facial expressions. Keep them cool and neutral."

"How's this?"

It must not have been good because Jim answered with "I wish we had more time to train you," Jim had said as Josiah and the task force had gone out the door. Jim and his wife Kat had joined fifteen minutes before "the mission." They are a husband and wife team who work together, taking down trafficking rings across the country. This was big time. Kat and Jim Gains had taken down America's Future, an organization that promised teens aging out of foster care an education and also asked them to do illegal things including murder. The organization had targeted Kat. She survived multiple assassination attempts before infiltrating the organization. Jim intercepted a bullet meant for Kat and nearly died. After exposing the leaders across the country, the organization imploded. I knew all this because I watched the news with Mom and Dad when it all happened. They didn't know I was watching, of course. I hid on the balcony and watched the big screen every night. That's what sleuths did, right? Now here they were in my living room! I couldn't believe it. Could I switch my career path and be Nancy Drew and an FBI agent?

When Jim finished giving instructions, I moved to the garage and waited for their exit. I followed them from a distance. They were so busy talking, I'm sure they didn't hear me tiptoeing behind them.

I had a clear view of the entire scene. The

pungent smoke from the fire made me sneeze. Before anyone could see me, I crawled on my stomach behind a small dune. I had worn all black. That's how you avoided being seen in the dark. The bonfire's radiant glow cast a haunting reflection of the college students, who moved with erratic dance moves on the sandy shore. Josiah looked relaxed on the outside as he approached the bandana-guy, but stomach was in knots. I knew because he threw up behind the dunes before he got to the bonfire. The sand beside me flew up in the air of its own volition. Then something wet and cold rooted around on my arm. I stifled a scream until I saw Rusty's shadowy form. He plopped himself down beside me lengthwise.

"This is a perfect place to set up, Rusty." Lemon's voice said from the darkness. She must have been wearing all black, too. I couldn't see her. She must have also covered her yellow hair.

FOR THE NEXT MINUTE, she unzipped bags and placed equipment in the sand.

"THIS IS SO EXCITING. I rarely get to do surveillance," she said to Rusty. She reached over to pat him on the head. Only problem is, she reached too far and patted me on the head.

She pulled her hand back as if she had touched a hot burner.

"Who is there?" Lemon said. I didn't say a word.

She exhaled. "It must be someone Rusty knows," she said, more to herself than me.

"It's Sera," I whispered.

"Sera, what are you?.... Nevermind. Just stay here with me." She continued setting up equipment and within minutes, we could hear the conversation around the bonfire crystal clear. Plus we could watch it on a little tv monitor.

AFTER FIVE MINUTES, Kat and Jim joined us. Jim folded himself like an accordion into the sand dune.

"PUT THIS BLACK BEANIE ON, JIM," Kat whispered, trying to conceal his fiery red hair.

"KAT, THIS IS SERA," Lemon whispered.

"Oh, the Nancy Drew girl," she smiled and her teeth glowed in the dark. "We should have a conversation about mysteries later. But for now. Watch and learn."

Funny, she was an adult, but she didn't scold me for being here. She didn't tell me to go back. In fact, she seemed totally fine with me being here. Maybe some day she'd let me be a part of her team.

THE THOUGHT of toasting marshmallows and tasting their gooey sweetness around the bonfire crossed my mind. The event seemed to be harmless. Did we bring the FBI here for no reason? Sure, they drank some beer. Most of the students talked and joked around, including the undercover task force teens. Damica seemed to talk to everyone, joking around and asking questions here and there. There was no interrogation. No swat team. No one looked as if they were being kidnapped or trafficked. It just seemed like a party.

"What time is it?" I rubbed my eyes.

"It's one in the morning," she said.

"Did I fall asleep?"

"For an hour."

"SO NOTHING HAPPENED?" I asked.

"What?" she said as she packed up her equipment.

"I mean it was just a party."

"Everything is not what it seems," she said with a laugh.

Lemon carefully stowed her camera, tripod, and lenses into her bag, ready to leave. Kat and Jim had left an hour before. Maybe their hasty departure meant they'd been called here for nothing. Lemon patiently watched as each teenager and member of the undercover team left the area before finally rising and stretching. "Let's go kiddo, I need to get you home."

"What happens next?"

"I think you get in trouble," she said.

"I mean with the case."

"Well, Damica gives a report. We watch and listen to the captured footage. The task force reports what they learned. Then figure out the next steps."

Chapter 6

"Young lady, what do you think you were doing sneaking out and following them?" Dad said as he opened the door, after I typed in the code.

Lemon was right. I was in trouble.

"Mr. Craven, she was with me. We hid in the dunes. She was perfectly safe," Lemon said, and Rusty barked in agreement.

"Thank you, Lemon. I'll take it from here." Dad said. He pulled me in the door and shut it in Lemon's face.

"Sera, I know you love sleuthing, but the FBI is here. For gosh sake. This is serious stuff."

"I know, dad. I'm sorry." I said, but I wasn't and he knew it.

"What are we going to do with you, squirt?" Josiah put in his own two cents. Another phrase I learned from dad. That means give your opinion.

Mom sipped a cup of coffee on the sectional. She observed quietly, her eyes focused on the tense exchange between my dad and me. She stood and hugged me. "I love you, Sera. You are precious and important. We just don't want anything to happen to you."

Sam, Isabella, and Mandy must have been in bed. The house was oddly quiet.

"Mom, I promise I won't do anything stupid," I said while patting her on the back.

"Now go to bed," Dad said. "We'll talk more about this in the morning."

My shoulders slumped. That meant this wasn't over. I would get a consequence in the morning. Vacation ruined. And the FBI was here. I didn't want to miss out on anything. How could I convince them it was okay to help? I was a sleuth. I knew what I was doing.

Sam met me in the hallway, "Sera, I can't believe you sneaked out and went to the bonfire! That's so cool." He smacked me on the back.

"No, it's not, Sam. It was dangerous," Josiah said. "This is serious, guys, not some Nancy Drew book."

Something was wrong. Josiah said nothing like that about my sleuthing or Nancy Drew books. His furrowed brow and clenched jaw hinted at his anger towards me. Or maybe he thought I didn't know what I was doing.

"I didn't go to the bonfire. I was with Lemon, surveilling." I said. "I'm going to bed." I tiptoed into my room and grabbed my pjs.

"You're back," Mandy whispered. "Dad was so

mad! Agent Kat from the FBI, texted Mom and said you were with Lemon."

"Really?" I said.

"Yeah, that's the only reasons dad didn't come looking for you," Isabella said as she sat up and rubbed the sleep out of her eyes.

"You have to tell us everything," Mandy said. She grabbed her pillow and hugged it.P

"Let me change and brush my teeth first," I said. It took me a while to process that Kat, the leader of a task force, had supported me. That was unfamiliar territory for me. My sleuthing was either mocked or considered cute by most people. Why was Kat standing up for me? And Lemon?

I slipped into my cozy pajamas, ready to spill all the details to Mandy and Isabella. But when I flipped off the bathroom light and stepped back into the bedroom, it was dark and quiet. The clock said 2:00. Isabella snorted and then settled into breathing in a steady cadence. Mandy rolled over, moaned, and went back to sleep.

The gentle rustle of the sheets and the faint creak of the mattress greeted me as I settled in. I could tell them everything in the morning. This gave me more time to think.

The next thing I knew, Mom was shaking me. "Sera, come have some breakfast. Dad and I need to talk to you."

I scanned the room. Mandy and Isabella were gone. Their beds were made.

I changed into a plaid skirt, sleeveless blouse, and penny loafers.

The rich, comforting aroma of freshly brewed coffee wafted towards me, awakening my senses.

"Yes, strong coffee, not the weak stuff dad makes," I slurped in a huge gulp.

"Hey, watch it squirt. You are already in hot water." Josiah said as he slid into the chair beside me.

"Where is everyone?" I said.

"At the beach with dad. You and I have somewhere to be in half an hour, so eat up." Josiah said while ruffling my hair.

"What?" I looked at Mom as she handed me a plate of French Toast.

"Kat and Lemon stopped by this morning. It seems they would like you to come to their meeting today."

"What? An FBI meeting?" I said, jumping up.

"Eat first," Mom said, while handing me a fork.

"Does this mean I'm not in trouble?" I asked. I shoved a bite of French Toast in my mouth and took a swig of coffee. I wanted to finish and leave before Mom changed her mind.

"I didn't say that," Mom said. "We'll discuss that later."

Twenty-five minutes later, Josiah and I walked into the lobby of the Sand Dune Hotel.

"It's the Palm Tree Conference Room," he said to me and to himself.

I suggested smoothing my plaid skirt. "Let's ask at the desk."

"Okay, but let me talk," Josiah said.

I could almost taste the anticipation in the air, as we awaited entry into the conference room. Josiah wasn't very good at sleuthing. He hadn't asked the bald man at the desk with a crooked nose and cinnamon-colored eyes questions other than - "Where is the Palm Tree Conference Room?" I still wasn't sure if he fit on the bad-guy list. He had a crooked nose, but his eyes were nice and his teeth were white and straight.

"Sera," Lemon yelled from across the room. She was wearing pink plaid clam diggers and a sleeveless pink blouse. Her lipstick matched her blouse. She knew how to dress like a sleuth. "Come over here!"

With a determined march, Josiah headed toward Jim and the other guys on the task force.

Lemon, Kat, and Damica, the profiler, leaned over a large screen.

"Aww, our Nancy Drew is here," Kat said. "I'm so glad you could come help." She slipped an arm around my shoulder and gave me a side hug. "I've heard good things about your sleuthing skills."

Two of the girls came and joined us. One with beautiful coffee-colored skin and spiral curls. The petite girl's slight frame made her appear like a little ballerina, bouncing gracefully on her tiptoes.

"Sera, meet my kids, Joyce and Jordan. Girls, this is Sera, our Nancy Drew."

Joyce and Jordan both said "Hello," and then leaned in toward the screen.

"Do we have anything yet?" Jordan asked. "I'm

ready for a fight. I'll take them down with my own hands."

I would sort out my confusion about the family relationships later. I leaned in and watched the screen.

The fire blazed in the middle. Laughter and animated chatter echoed from the illuminated faces, contrasting with the subdued whispers from those in the shadows. I looked for clues.

"There!" I shouted.

"What do you see?" Lemon asked.

"That man with the hat." I pointed towards him. He works here at the hotel.

"Good eye, Sera," Kat said. "He's one of ours. Sometimes hotel managers are part of human trafficking rings. In order to take control, we made the decision to plant our own manager. Maybe someone from the ring will approach him."

Kat was cool. She talked to me as if I were an adult. She didn't make fun of me. It felt like a compliment when she called me Nancy Drew. She tied up her chestnut hair on top of her head and wore a sundress and cardigan with sandals.

Jim declared that we would be taking a lunch break after we had watched and listened to the footage for another two hours.

Josiah appeared at my side. "Let's go squirt. That's enough for the day."

"Oh, wait, at least eat lunch with us," Kat said. "Lunch is when everyone talks!"

"I'll have to ask my mom." I said.

"I'll ask her," Kat said. She pulled out her phone and typed out a text.

A few seconds later, she said, "Your Mom says 'yes', just come home after."

Not only did I get to watch surveillance videos, now I was going to eat lunch with the FBI task force.

Josiah joined the guys. I sat between Damica and Jordan, with Kat and Lemon across from me. I was in heaven.

Chapter 7

"So, Sera, what sparked your interest in Nancy Drew?" Kat asked.

"When I was in the orphanage someone donated a few Nancy Drew books and I read them over and over."

"That's interesting, but there has to be more to the story." Damica prodded.

"Well, I started solving mysteries and I'm good at it. Sometimes I got myself in trouble though." I decided I better add that because Damica is a profiler. Maybe she can read my mind.

"Oh, me too," Kat said. "I did a bunch of stupid stuff on my first human trafficking case." She smiled at me.

"Did she ever," Damica said with a giggle.

"I've not heard this story," Lemon said. "I've only heard about how great you are." Lemon leaned in.

I couldn't believe grown-ups were talking about their mistakes. We kids always felt as if we needed to not make mistakes. As if when we grew up, we wouldn't make any more mistakes. At least that's what I thought.

Kat leaned in and so did the other ladies. "Well, there was this guy named Devon. He was in Green Pines, the same group home I was a teen. And he was bad news. When he grew up, he started trafficking teens aging out of the system. Then he decided to kill me…." she took a sip from her tiny cup of coffee.

"Get to the good stuff," Jordan said. "Like you got Damica kidnapped, Bennie shot, and Maryanne kidnapped."

"I think that's enough for now," a low voice said.

"Oh, Jim, we're just telling Sera about my first case," Kat said.

"Could I talk to you for a minute?" Jim said. He pulled on her elbow.

He moved about five feet away from the table. "Kat, she is a child. Why are you telling her all this? You're going to scare her."

"Jim, she's not just a child. She's like me."

Jim's tousled hair resembled the wild, untamed strands of sea grass swaying in the wind. "What do you mean?"

"Well, she was in an orphanage most of her life. None of this," she waved an arm around the room, "is new to her."

"That may be," Jim said, "but maybe you should tone it down a bit."

I stood up and walked over to Jim, and studied him.

"What are you doing?" Kat asked.

"Trying to decide if he should go on my bad guy list."

Kat giggled. Jim gave her a stern look.

"I mean," I stood on my tiptoes. I needed a stepladder to reach his red hair. "This is a bad guy trait. Messy hair."

"Time to go, squirt," Josiah said, pulling me by the elbow. "Sorry, sir." Josiah said, backing away with me in tow.

"But, I'm not finished," I said to Josiah, stumbling back on him.

"Let's pack up your lunch and take it with us."

"All ready for you," Lemon said and handed me a paper plate with saran wrap over it.

"We'll talk more later," Jordan said with a grin.

"Bye!" I said, waving at the group and wishing I could spend the rest of the day with them. I looked around and saw familiar faces. A sense of belonging washed over me. These were my people. As I stepped out of the conference room, I looked back. Jordan raised a fisted hand and said, "Power to the People, Sera." Yes, these were my people.

On our way out of the hotel, I stopped at the bathroom. When I came out, Josiah was talking to one guy from the task force.I forgot my clue book. I retraced my steps, silently slipping back into the conference room, hoping not to draw attention. I didn't want Josiah to grab it for me or tell me to wait until later. When I entered the conference room, lunch was being cleared away and people were talking in little groups.

I saw Jim, Damica, and Kat in a corner and walked towards them. Jim had his back to me.

"I guess she is like you," Jim said.

"Jim, sharing our stories with Sera will help her, not hurt her. She needs to know that grownups mess up too." Kat said.

"We know some of her story." Damica said. "We know that she almost fell victim to trafficking." She knows a lot more than you think, Jim."

"What about all this Nancy Drew stuff?" Jim asked.

"It's her coping mechanism," Damica said.

What? No, it's not. Why would she say that? I turned on my heel and ran out of the room. I thought these were my people. I was wrong. Damica was just like the therapist Mom had taken me to. She had told me I was safe now, and I needed to let go of this fantasy. It is time to let go of Nancy Drew. Dress normally. Act like other little girls.

My vision was blurred by tears streaming down my face. I ran past Josiah and out the front door of the hotel. I kept running all the way home.

With a loud slam, I closed the door and hurriedly made my way to my room, where I threw myself on the bed. I wasn't helping them anymore. They thought I wasn't good enough. I felt broken. I couldn't sleuth.

"Hey, squirt, that was some sprint." Josiah said from the doorway. "I got your clue book for you."

He set the clue notebook on my bed and sat down. "What's up? First, you want to stay and then run out of there like you are being chased."

"I don't want to help them anymore," I said.

"Okay, that's fine," he said. "Is there a reason?"

I shoved my face deeper into the pillow.

"Don't want to talk about it. Got it," he stood and shut the door. Then he opened it a crack and said, "Let's go down to the beach, Sera, don't let this ruin your vacation. Whatever it is," he said the last sentence more to himself than me, I could tell.

Right then, I decided to solve the case on my own. I would prove to Jim who I was definitely adding to my bad guy list, Damica too. Even though she is pretty and has lovely blonde curls. When I solved the case, they wouldn't make fun of my "coping mechanism." They would know I was the real deal.

I raised myself up and wiped my eyes. "Okay, Josiah, I'll get ready."

Chapter 8

Before entering the ocean, I soaked up the sun to warm up at the beach. I sat alone, staring at the empty water bottle in my hand, lost in thought, contemplating my strategy before approaching Sam, Isabella, and Mandy. Plus, I wasn't sure how much I wanted to tell them. If Sam got grumpy- old-man on us, then he would pout and tell dad. I had to proceed with caution. I was going to solve this whole trafficking thing and show them. But first, I was going to splash in the waves!

Isabella, Sam, Isabella, and I spend the remainder of the day riding waves and burying each other in the sand. Later in the afternoon, dad helped us build a huge sandcastle with a moat. Josiah pitched in.

"Glad to see you've cheered up, squirt," he said as he patted the sand around the moat that had just filled up with water.

"Sera says she isn't helping the task force anymore," Sam said. "Did something happen?"

"So now we have no case to solve," said Mandy with a frown.

"What about the break-outs?" Isabella asked.

"You mean break-ins?" Sam said, smacking her wet head. Tiny drops of water dripped down her shoulders. Isabella tensed and balled her fists.

"That's enough, Sam," Dad said.

"I'm mad, Dad. Sera has this chance to work with the FBI and she blows it. Like does she know how cool that would be. I thought we could all help."

"Sam, this is serious business. I'm glad Sera doesn't want to help," Mom said from her chair. She lowered her book and smiled.

"Hey, there's George," Mandy said. "Let's go question him."

Sam threw a handful of sand in the moat. "I'm not helping," he said as he stomped up the beach. "Can I go back to the beach house?" he asked. He was in grumpy-old-man mode. I was not letting him in on my secret mission.

"I'll join you," Mom said to Sam, popping out of her seat.

"Come on, guys, I'll go with you to talk to George," Josiah said.

"I guess I'll gather everything up by myself," Dad said.

"We'll help, dad," I said. "We'll be right back."

George was setting up a chair and pulling out his gear. "Hello," he said.

"Hi, remember us?" I asked.

"Of course, you like to interrupt fishermen," he said with a frown.

"Sir, we just want to ask you one question," Mandy said.

"Yes, have you seen anyone auspicious? There have been some break-ins." Isabella said with a smile.

At least she got half of it right.

"Oh, that. I thought you kids were going to ask me for money or something," he smiled, and his entire demeanor changed. "No, I haven't."

"Thanks for your help," I said.

"Let's go help dad," Josiah said and we followed him down the beach like little ducks in a row.

"Hey, wait," I turned to see George running up the beach towards us. He sprinted with surprising agility. His previously slouched posture had transformed into a young and athletic stance.

When he got closer, Josiah stood protectively in front of us.

"Just want to ask you kids a quick question." He wasn't even out of breath. He pulled the latest version of a smartphone out of his vest pocket and pulled up a photo. "Have you run into this guy?"

Bandana-guy. What was going on here?

"Yes," Josiah said. "But I don't want to have anything to do with him." he added, turning away and pushing us towards dad.

"Good. Stay away from him and keep the girls away from him." he turned. I glanced over my shoulder. He ran back to his chair.

"Josiah, don't you think there is something weird about George?" I asked.

"He's just trying to watch out for us, I think," said Josiah while shrugging his shoulders. His voice carried a tone of disbelief, with a hint of skepticism in his words.

"His fishing vest was new. So were his pants," I said. "Grandpa's are old and tattered," I added.

"Maybe he bought them for this trip," Mandy suggested.

"Yep. You may be right. But did you see him run? He didn't run like an old man. He ran like you, Josiah." I said, straightening my bathing suit skirt.

"You know, you're right Sera, you may be on to something," Josiah said with a grin. Then his face became serious. "Stay away from him, girls."

"And his phone," Isabella added. "Josiah, your phone isn't that new."

"Plus Grandpa doesn't have a smartphone at all." I continued.

Josiah stopped. "What are you saying, Sera?"

"I don't know. He's just not who he says he is." I waved at dad and ran to help him gather the towels and beach toys. Whoever George was, he wasn't a bad guy. He tried to keep us from harm.

As we carried the cooler, beach bags, and toys back up to the beach house, we ran into Lemon.

"Hi, guys!" She said as Rusty strained at his leash. "Sera, are you coming to the evening meeting?"

"Sera has decided not to help," Dad said. "Thank you for the invitation."

"That's too bad, we were just getting to know her."

You mean finding out more ways to make fun of me behind my back? Nope. I wasn't going back.

"We'll be at the hotel at 6pm if you change your mind." Then she lowered her voice to a whisper. "I'll be doing surveillance again on the beach." She turned and looked at Josiah. "Did you get invited to the party tonight at 8?"

"No, I don't think I'll get invited to anymore. They weren't happy that I didn't bring my sisters. That puts me on the blacklist."

"Okay. Makes sense. Stay safe then. Don't go." and then she trotted off down the boardwalk in her hot pink tank and clam diggers as if we had just been talking about the weather.

A plan was forming in my mind. Josiah had to go to the party. I had to go with him. I had to solve this. What could go wrong? Lemon would be on surveillance. She would watch while I solved the whole thing and took down the trafficking ring. Then Kat, Jim, and Damica would know my sleuthing was my superpower, not a silly little coping mechanism.

Chapter 9

How was I going to convince Josiah to go to the party and let me join him? I couldn't involve Sam or the girls. They would certainly tell on me. Dinner was winding down. The sound of the coffee machine hummed as mom and dad discussed heading to the beach to enjoy the gentle waves crashing on the shore. Sam, Isabella, and Mandy were talking about watching a movie and making popcorn.

The sun would go down soon. Suddenly, the image of tiny, scuttling sand crabs emerged in my mind. The glowing crabs we had chased the first night.

Mom was pouring the freshly brewed coffee into a carafe. "Hey, mom can I go watch the sand crabs and take some pictures like Lemon did?"

"You'll have to have someone with you," Mom said. "Or stay right by your dad and me."

That definitely wouldn't work.

Fear consumed me as I envisioned Sam and the girls wanting to go, sabotaging my entire plan.

"I'm not going," Sam said. "I'm too tired. Plus I'm still mad at you Sera. You ruined everything."

The girls were siding with him. Mandy watched as the bag of popcorn spun inside the microwave, the steam building up against the plastic. Isabella crossed her arms and said, "Yeah, Sam is right. You ruined our sluicing opportunity."

Sam didn't correct her. Instead, he grabbed a bowl out of the cabinet and moved to wait for the microwave to beep.

Sam and Isabella getting along was a miracle and right on time. Relief washed over me like a gentle wave. All of them were mad at me and wouldn't follow. Now, to convince Josiah to take me out.

"Josiah," I said with my best smile.

Josiah draped himself over the comfy chair in the family room, studying his phone.

"Yeah, squirt?"

"Would you take me out to watch the ghost crabs?"

"Sera, we've had a long day," he said. I knew he was serious because he called me by my name. There was no chance he would change his mind. Not once he called me by my name.

My shoulders slumped. I was failing. I wouldn't be able to take down a human trafficking ring because I was too young to go out on my own. How stupid was that? Then I thought about Nancy Drew. How many times had she gone off on her own and not told her dad? Sometimes things went wrong, but she always came out on the other side. She always solved the mystery.

I guess I was doing this on my own. I went up to the girl's room and packed a backpack with a flashlight, water bottle, and a camera. Mom and dad had left for the beach. The rest of the family and Mandy were settling down in the family room with popcorn and a movie. I just needed to sneak past them.

I crawled on all fours behind the sectional and headed for the backdoor. Everyone was so engrossed in the movie, they didn't notice me. Once outside, the next hurdle I had was to find the party and make sure dad and mom didn't see me on the beach. Mom and dad were watching the sunset like it was a great mystery movie. I slipped past them, making sure I stayed about twenty feet behind them. The sandcrabs scattered in my path. I mimicked their brisk, darting steps and scurried across the sandy shore. After a few minutes, darkness and a few ghost crabs surrounded me. As far as I could see, there was no light of a bonfire. Did I get the time right?

I sat down on a dune to form a new plan. While I sat listening to the waves crashing on the shore, bandana-guy ran four feet in front of me. Spraying sand my way. He must not have seen me. I scooted back even further. He was running from something or someone. That wasn't the gait of a jogger working out. A second later, fisherman George ran by. I hopped to my feet and followed. It was hard to keep up. I was breathing hard, but not so hard that I sounded as loud as what I was hearing. It sounded like two deer were snorting in my ears on either side. A shiver ran down my spine as I resisted the urge to look behind me. Plus, if I turned, I would lose my balance and fall.

"Just stop, man. I don't even know your sister!" Bandana-guy yelled. He had stopped running and turned to face fisherman George.

George reached in his vest and pulled out a gun.

"You're going to tell me where she is or that's the last thing you're ever going to…" He paused and turned toward me.

I dropped to the ground and prayed the darkness would cover me.

"Why did you follow me?" he said to the darkness behind me.

I didn't turn but kept my eyes on bandana-guy. He was standing now. George was so busy talking to whoever was behind us he was going to let him get away. Experiencing the loss of a "sister" was something I understood. I had no time to think. Instead, I acted. In one fluid motion, I stood, ran, and plowed into bandana-guy while yelling, "GEORGE" at the same time.

Bandana-guy cussed and grabbed me by my hair. He pulled me up to my feet like a puppet on a string. I screamed and kicked him in the shins.

A gunshot rang out and whizzed past my arm. It stung like ten wasps. I screamed for the second time, and my body went limp. Bandana-guy dropped me.

"You killed a kid, man!" He didn't sound tough anymore. He sounded like a scared kid.

I grabbed my arm. Sticky oozy blood covered my hand. I didn't speak. I moaned in pain and waited.

"Isn't that what you do?" George said, advancing toward me. "Kid, are you okay?"

"No man, I don't kill kids. This is crazy. I didn't sign up for this." Bandana-guy kneeled down and pulled out his phone. He punched in some numbers.

"911, what's your emergency?"

"Someone shot a kid on the beach. Get here fast. She's bleeding." He gave them a mile marker,and street name,and hung up.

George was beside me now, checking my arm with the flashlight on his phone.

"I'm so sorry, kid. I told you to stay away from this guy."

"Sera," two familiar voices shouted. I leaned back and everything went dark.

Chapter 10

I awoke and made an effort to remember what happened before I blacked out. The air was filled with the scent of antiseptic. Stiff white sheets held me snugly in place. An IV line protruded from my arm.

"I got shot," I said to myself.

As Mom rushed towards me, the surrounding room seemed to blend into a hazy blur.

"Sera, you're awake! How are you honey?" she said, giving me a gentle hug.

"I got shot, mom. I'm sorry. That was so stupid."

A tear dripped down my cheek. "I sneaked out and I followed bandana-guy and fisherman George who isn't a fisherman at all. He's trying to find his sister."

"We know, honey, calm down. You need to rest." Dad said.

"We heard it all," Josiah said from the corner.

"Yeah," said Sam. "We saw you get shot, Sera," and let out a guttural sob.

"You guys were the ones following me? The ones George yelled at?"

"Yes, I saw you sneaking out." Josiah said. "I grabbed Sam and we followed you. Next thing I knew, you were in the middle of … and you…" He stopped there and sucked in a deep breath. "Squirt, you have to stop doing dangerous stuff. Like you could be dead right now."

They didn't understand sleuthing. Sometimes Nancy Drew got hurt, but she was always okay in the end. There's always a risk involved in sleuthing. It's in all the books. My arm was throbbing now, so I didn't want to explain it. I'd do it later.

"I'm tired, Mom, and hungry."

Sam and Josiah emerged from the corner and made their way out of the room with a shuffle. Sam wiped his eyes.

"I'll get you some food," Mom said.

"And a cup of coffee?" I asked.

"After you sleep," Dad said.

I ate the turkey wrap my mom gave me and then fell into a deep sleep.

When I woke, dad was the only other one in the room. He was snoring in the chair. Then a yellow head peaked in the door.

"Hey Sera, can I come in?"

"Lemon!" I whispered.

Lemon entered, bearing gifts. The sweet scent of freshly baked cupcakes mingled with the crisp fragrance of the new book. Not a Nancy Drew, but a mystery.

"I'm so glad you're going to be okay," she said. "What you did was dangerous."

Dad stood and stretched, "Hey Lemon. Can you stay with Sera while I get this kiddo a cup of coffee?"

"Coffee?" Lemon said, puzzled.

"She has mature tastes."

"Yes, you remind me of my wife," Agent Gaines's flaming red hair appeared followed by his scarecrow-like body.

"I do?" I asked. "But I'm mad at you. You think I can't sleuth." I said, turning my head toward him.

Next, Kat, the wife of Agent Gains, arrived with a bunch of daisies and a pile of Nancy Drew books. Damica followed with a plastic coffee cup and a box of muffins.

"Oh, I leave for five minutes, and you have a party," Dad said from the doorway. "Sorry, kiddo, they only have regular coffee here, no espresso here."

The aromatic scent of freshly pressed espresso wafted from the cup, filling the air around Damica. "Got you covered, kiddo."

"Dad, I don't want these people here. Except Lemon."

"Don't be rude, honey. They came to check on you," Dad said.

"And to tell you something," Agent Gaines said.

"I don't want to talk to you. You guys made fun of me. You said my sleuthing was a coping mechanism." I turned and shoved my head into the pillow. Salty tears dripped into my mouth. They tasted bitter. I hated this feeling. You're not good enough. You'll never be good enough. You don't matter.

"Could I talk to her?" It was Kat's voice. Dad must have said yes. I heard the coffee cup clunk down on the tray. Then the shuffling of feet leaving the room.

"You made fun of me." I said into the pillow so it sounded more like "U mud fin of muhhh."

"No, I didn't."

"What about the coping skills?"

"Coping skills are a strength. You know what my coping skills are?"

"You have them too?"

"Of course."

"What are they?" I sat up now and hugged the pillow.

"First. Quoting murder mysteries. Out loud. It's so embarrassing sometimes. But they help me process."

"Oh," I didn't know what to say.

"You want to know another one I have? I think my husband mentioned you reminded me of him?"

"Yes," I didn't know why. We looked nothing alike. I was dark. She was fair.

"I try to solve everything on my own. I rush ahead alone and don't ask for help."

I repeated the word "Oh. Like I did last night."

"Exactly. Every time I try to do it alone, you know what happens?"

"Nancy Drew does it alone."

"When she does, what happens?"

"She ends up kidnapped, locked in cellars, and other stuff like that."

"Right she gets herself in trouble. Remember - Nancy is a great sleuth but she's not perfect. Think through some situations you just told me about. And then think of how she could have done them differently."

I thought for a minute and then said, "Did you ever get shot?"

"You want to know the worst thing I did? Got my husband shot. He almost died."

"And that's enough," Dad said from the doorway.

Kat stood. "I'm sorry. I didn't mean to overstep."

Mom breezed in between them. "You didn't. You're fine. Carry on. Ben, can I talk to you outside?" Mom pulled Dad's shirt sleeve and Kat sunk heavily into the chair.

"I did it again," Kat said, hanging her head. "I shared too much."

I watched through the crack in the door as Mom and Dad argued in the hallway.

"She experienced a major trauma," Dad said. His jaw clenched, veins protruding on his temple, a grimace etched on his face. "And this FBI agent is talking about horrific things."

"Ben, Sera has already been through horrific things. It's better that she knows other people have too."

"She was in an orphanage, Clare. How bad could that have been? As far as we know, no one carried firearms in the orphanage and shot children."

"Ben, I know you know some of my past. You know I lived in a group home. Group homes provide food and shelter, yes. Unfortunately, they also are breeding grounds for sexual abuse and other traumas.Perhaps I should share some of my past, painting a clearer picture."

"Maybe you need to talk to your daughter and share your common denominator of your trauma history and how it affects you now," another voice said. Then silence. Followed by whispering I couldn't understand.

Mom stepped back in the room. "Sera, we need to talk." Damica followed, pulling a chair up to the bed for Mom.

Sipping on my espresso, I waited for what would come next.

For the next half hour, Kat, Damica, and Mom talked while I listened in wide-eyed wonder. Evidently, everyone had their own coping strategies. They were not a vulnerability or something to feel ashamed of. They were proof that you were not only a survivor, but words the pastor had used in church - more than a conqueror.

A feeling of relief washed over me, followed by a wave of exhaustion. Mom noticed my eyelids fluttering and ushered everyone out of the room. Just as I was about to drift off to sleep, a massive head appeared above me. A fair and freckled face was framed by flaming hair standing on end.

"Kat, I wanted to fill her in on the case."

My eyes popped open. He leaned closer, blurry.

"Jim, let's do it later. Let her sleep." Kat's voice echoed from the hallway.

It felt like heavy weights were attached to my eyes. I had happy dreams of working for the FBI, the youngest agent in history. I ran between Agents Kat and Jim Gaines, with a theme song playing in the background.

Chapter 11

I spent a few nights in the hospital. The doctor told Mom and Dad the bullet had "grazed" my arm. Concern etched deep lines on his face, his brows furrowing as he contemplated my mental well-being and the risk of infection. My mental state wasn't in any danger. In fact, my wound not only made me feel like a real sleuth, but it also connected me to Mom and the FBI agents in a new way.

I had no idea that other people used coping mechanisms. The staff at the orphanage didn't have the time or resources to teach us how to cope with being orphaned. Their main goal was to help us survive - literally provide food, water, and shelter. Plus, if possible, get us adopted into a home. Not even a good home - just a home that could provide an education and a way out of the poverty we lived in. Camila said the Colombian hosting program was a God-send. She encouraged us kids to learn English. Some kids had no interest in trying. They were so stuck they couldn't imagine a different life. The Nancy Drew books had been a portal into a different world for me. Through the books, I learned what a loving family relationship could look like. What I also learned - sleuthing. Damica had shared with me how it helped me into the life I was building with my new family, but warned me, like Kat had, that Nancy was human. Nancy made mistakes, especially when she went out on her own. I thought about all the things the grown-ups had said. It made me feel better. Stronger. I couldn't put it into words.

Mandy, Isabella, Sam, and Josiah had spent a lot of time with me. The sound of our laughter and playful banter echoed throughout the room, blending with the background music from the movies. During one of our rousing games of charades, the doctor had peeked in.

"Looks like a slumber party!" he said with a chuckle. He rubbed his hand over his droopy eyes and turned to the nurse. "Janice, let the Cravens know Sera can go home." Then he checked my arm. "Everything looks good, Sera"

When he left the room, Sam said, "I can't believe you're going to have a scar from a BULLET. That's so cool."

Josiah rapped him on the head with a Nancy Drew book. "No, Sam, it's not. Josiah rapped him on the head with a Nancy Drew book and said, "No, Sam, it's not. She could have been killed."

"Is operation 'watch Sera at all times' starting now?" Isabella asked.

"You weren't supposed to say that! It's a secret, covert op!" Sam said, glaring at her. "Plus it's WSAAT. You're supposed to say WSAAT!"

"It's okay, Sam. Sera is a sleuth. She would have figured it out," Mandy offered.

"That's a cool acrostic. I like it! Sam, did you think of that?"

His head popped up, "yes, I did! You really like it?"

"Yes, I do!" Everyone smiled.

Mom and Dad filled out the final discharge paperwork. The sad part about my injury and the hospital stay -it had eaten up two days of our vacation. We only had a few left. If I was going to help take down the human trafficking ring, it had to be quick.

The next morning, Kat, Jim, and Lemon showed up at the beach house. Dad said he had invited them so he could hear what was going on. And I'm one hundred percent sure he wanted to have some more control over what I was doing. Nancy Drew's dad gave her advice.

Mom carried a tray of mugs and a carafe of coffee into the family room. Mandy followed her with a tray of muffins while Josiah handled the water pitcher. Isabella snuggled into the chair and a half with me. Dad looked stern and serious as he poured himself a cup of coffee.

"Ben, our guests," Mom said.

"Oh, yes." He hadn't waited on them, which

meant he was in serious-mode. Instead, he sipped his coffee and stared at Agent Jim Gaines.

Mom stepped in and poured the coffee. Mandy offered muffins and then everyone sat.

There was a knock at the door. Sam jumped up and answered. Damica stumbled in carrying a whiteboard, easel and bag.

"Sorry, I'm late. I had to stop and pick up Kat's whiteboard."

Jim and Kat stood. Within thirty seconds, they had everything set up.

"This is what we know," Kat began. She turned and wrote on the board. I was so excited. I wasn't the only one who used a whiteboard. I was a real sleuth. Visions of me in running between the Gains Agents with theme music flashed across my head again.

"Wait," dad said. "I thought this meeting was about how much Sera was going to be involved in this investigation." He stood up. "My daughter got shot."

"Ben…" Mom said, tugging on his arm. His face was hot and angry, like salsa.

"Oh, I didn't realize…" Kat said.

"Okay," Damica said. "That's a good place to start. What are the parameters? We understand you are upset. No one here wants your daughter in harm's way. Or any of these other kids." She swept her arm around the room for emphasis.

"Sera, you cannot go out on your own. Or any ops that will put you in danger." He said. But he wasn't looking at me. He was looking at Jim. Pointing at Jim. His finger moved forward with each word.

"Ben, I would never send your daughter out alone or into the path of danger."

"Dad," I said. "I went by myself."

"Do we agree to that parameter?" Damica said, grabbing a marker. She wrote on the board, "Sera," and then listed all the kids' names. She clarified that putting them in danger was not acceptable.

"In…" Dad didn't get to finish his sentence.

"Ben, no one can promise that nothing bad will happen," Mom cut in.

Dad sat down and grabbed his coffee. "Okay," he said. He gripped his coffee tighter and his knuckles turned white.

"Dad, you don't need to worry about Sera being alone. We," Isabella interjected, and she pointed to Mandy, Sam, Josiah, and then herself, "are doing WHAT's UP!"

"You mean WSAAT," Sam said.

"This sounds interesting," Agent Jim said. "An acrostic?"

"Yep," Sam said. He beamed. "I thought of it. It stands for Watch Sera At All Times."

"Perfect," said Kat. "Now can I get back to what we know?"

Before she could begin, a loud rapping at the door interrupted her. "Kat, Jim are you in there? Grandma said to come here."

Jim jumped up, followed by Dad. "Bennie," he said while ushering him into the living room.

"I can't go to work because Kat isn't working at

the library. Grandma said we needed a vacation. So, we are here. I'm here to help."

Kat introduced Bennie to everyone, while Jordan struggled in behind him, carrying a cooler.

"Mom, Meredith is setting up in her beach home. You know what that means. Everyone is going to be put to work until it is perfect. And apparently, I'm Bennie's pack horse." She set the cooler down.

When Kat introduced me, Bennie said, "You're the Nancy Drew Girl. Did you know Edward Stratemeyer had other ideas for names of the series - Diana Dare Stories, Helen Hale Stories…"

"Oh, I said."

"Oh, yeah. Meredith said they listened to Girl Sleuth, Nancy Drew and the Women Who Created Her on the way here," Jordan added. "I'm off, power to the female sleuth," she yelled as she exited, raising a fist for emphasis.

"Grandma said I needed to learn how to engage more socially, so I learned about Nancy Drew. You like her, right?Bennie didn't look at me when he directed the question to me. Instead, he looked out the picture window.

"Yes," I said.

"Then I did good, right Kat?" He swiveled his head towards her. "I like video games and graphic novels."

"Bennie, you did good. We are in the middle of a briefing. We can talk more about those things later."

Instead of sitting, Bennie stood in the middle of the room, rocking back and forth from side to side. I couldn't figure out his age. He shaved. He was an adult. But not an old adult like Mom and Dad. Probably older than Josiah by a few years. But he dressed like dad in pressed khakis cinched with a belt. His polo shirt tucked tightly in his khakis. But he acted like.. I don't know. Yes, I did. He was in survival mode. I saw other kids do that in the orphanage. Some of them rocked back and forth against the wall for hours, staring at nothing in particular. Other ones grasped at objects in front of them that weren't there.

"Would you like some coffee, Bennie?" Mom asked.

"No. Coffee tastes horrible. Coffee was discovered by a goat herder." He paused and then, as if he had practiced it, he said. "I don't like coffee but some people do. Kat does." He rocked back and forth more.

Jim stood. "Let's see what snacks you brought, Bennie."

Bennie stopped rocking and walked to the cooler. "Grandma said to share so she packed extra. Kids like Big Cups," he said as he lobbed one at Sam, Josiah, and the rest of us. "Orange soda is at the bottom."

Jim was rearranging the furniture. This was the weirdest meeting I had ever been to. Our family meetings were sometimes a little loud. Fun and frustrating. They were often about bedtimes, chores, and things we needed to work on. I glanced at Sam. He was eating this up. Isabella looked blank. Mandy is anxious. Josiah observed. He was a lot like Damica. I wondered if he would be a profiler one day.

"Bennie, here's a seat for you." Bennie tromped to the corner and plopped into the rattan chair. He unzipped his backpack and pulled out a gaming device. "I'll only put one earbud in so I can listen. I remember everything. That's why I'm on the task force. I hear and remember everything. Nancy Drew doesn't do that, but she…"

"Okay, Bennie…" Jim cut off.

Bennie kept talking. "In the early books, Nancy often wore glamorous heels and fashionable frocks while chasing suspects, climbing ladders and sleuthing for 'ghosts' in secret passageways.

Nancy's best friends, Bess Marvin and George Fayne, are cousins.

There are over 20 Nancy Drew computer games. There I ended on a positive note," he said and then looked down at his game.

Kat and Damica looked unfazed. As if all of Bennie's behavior was perfectly normal.

"What we know," Kat began again. A soft rapping interrupted her.

Mom went to the door. "May I help you?" she said.

I leaned over and peered at the visitor. I stood. "Fisherman George!" I yelled.

Dad stood. "I thought you said Fisherman George was an old man."

"I said he looked like an old man," I said.

George sported a suntanned, muscular physique and was not much older than Josiah.

"That's right, Sera kept pointing out how he could run as fast as me," Josiah said.

"I'm sorry you got shot, Sera," George said. "I …" A tear dripped down his cheek.

Mom ushered him to the couch, and he sat down heavily and put his head into his hands.

"I didn't mean for any of this to happen. I just want to find my sister."

Chapter 12

Dad was on his feet, "So you shot Sera?" He yelled. His face was red and contorted.

"NO!" George looked up and shook his head violently. "I wouldn't shoot ... *sob*... man this is so embarrassing. Sorry for crying." He rubbed his face with his hands like a raccoon. "I'm just trying to find my sister."

Jim stepped between Dad and George. "Mr Craven, if you could just calm down. Let us share what we know. George did not shoot Sera. We don't have the man in custody. The shooter's absence leaves an empty space, like a missing puzzle piece, in the investigation. But we do have Brennan. He is telling us all he knows."

"Bandana-guy?" I asked.

"Yes. He called 911 when you got shot, Sera." Kat said.

"Yeah, he said 'No man, I don't kill kids. This is crazy. I didn't sign up for this,'" George said. I think he was going to tell me something. But there was someone behind him. That someone watched our entire conversation and shot Sera."

"I got shot once," Bennie yelled. "Lilith shot me. I told Kat she was a bad lady. She's in jail now."

"Bennie, you're yelling. Did you put both earbuds in?" Jim asked.

"Oh, sorry. I'll take one out." Bennie took an earbud out and went back to his game.

Dad sat down. Damica moved and sat next to George. She put an arm around his shoulder.

"Sera is good at finding sisters," Isabella offered. "She found me."

George looked at me. "But she's just a kid."

"Not just a kid. A sleuth. Top notch," Damica explained. "That's why we are meeting here. We're the FBI."

"Really?" George's gaze swept the room in disbelief.

"Yes, and this task force's speciality is taking down trafficking rings." Damica said with a smile as she patted him on the back.

"Oh, yeah. I recognize you." He looked at Kat. "You're on that show with Barbara on Best Broadcast News? Didn't you take down "America's Future?" He added.

"Okay,okay. Let's get down to business." Jim said, taking over. Kat's face was red.

To their surprise, Brennan (bandana-guy) had disclosed everything he knew, which wasn't much. He received payment for hosting parties on the beach and inviting teen and tween girls. According to him, "If some old man has a thing for young girls and wants to see them dance at a party, what's it to me? They paid me $5oo dollars per party during the tourist season."

Then, when he found out what was really going on, he tried to get out. He was threatened. They would kill him if he told the police that these young girls were vanishing. George's sister was one of these girls.

George had tried approaching some of the party hosts as himself and got nowhere except beat up and threatened himself. So he dressed up as an old fisherman. According to him, everyone ignored him, except us kids. He had learned when and where the parties were. He hid in the dunes and watched the operation, but hadn't gotten very far. So, he went after bandana-guy directly.

George's sister had disappeared a month earlier on a family vacation that he hadn't been able to attend because of college exams. George's sixteen-year-old brother had taken their fourteen-year-old sister, Grace, to a bonfire. His sister had disappeared. George's brother, Chance, was in a psychiatric ward. He couldn't live with the guilt and had tried to commit suicide. George's parents believed the worst, that someone had murdered Grace and left her for dead. They had hired private detectives after the police had failed to find her body.

"I'll visit your brother and see if I can help him," Damica promised.

"We'll find your sister," Kat said. "We just need to

figure out exactly how the operation works and follow the trail back to the head of the serpent."

"Understand this, I mean to arrive at the truth. The truth, however ugly in itself, is always curious and beautiful to seekers after it." Kat quoted.

No one commented on the fact that Kat was quoting murder mysteries. No one commented on the fact that Kat was quoting murder mysteries, accepting her coping mechanism for what it was. A way for her to process information.

"WHAT IF SHE'S DEAD?" George said.

"We don't know that she is. Most traffickers don't kill their victims. The victim is a valuable commodity." Bennie said.

"Is that true?" George said.

"Yes, the victim is worth more alive." Jim said.

"What we need is bait," Kat said. "I'm sure the organization is getting antsy. They might even pull up stakes and move on since bandana-guy turned himself in."

Dad stood. "Not my girls. They aren't going to be your bait."

"Of course not," Damica said. "We have agents for this sort of thing. Last year, I went undercover as a college student."

"Oh," Dad said and sat down. "How old are you?"

"Ben, you don't ask a lady her age." Mom said with a laugh.

"I'm 37," she said. "We sometimes recruit agents who look younger than they are. Or who can blend in."

"We'll need an older male 'sibling' and a young 'female' that seems to be what they look for." Jim said.

"Let me look at some agent files and see who we can bring in," Kat said. "I'll need Maryanne to help me with this one."

The meeting ended with a plan in place. Kat had called Maryanne, and they had talked for a few minutes.

I was in awe. My mouth was hanging open. I could feel it. I was in the middle of an FBI meeting. I was included. They were sharing the whole op right in front of us. No one questioned me being there.

Chapter 13

I tiptoed on the sand, imitating Lemon. She had given me a small camera and told me to take pictures of anything I thought could be a clue.

I couldn't believe it. Here I was a girl-sleuth, working with the FBI!

Isabella had cried because she couldn't come. "I'm supposed to watch Sera," she had said. "The last time I didn't watch her, she got shot."

"Kat and Lemon will watch her, Isabella," Josiah had said. "She will be safe."

Isabella had stomped up to the girl's room. Damica followed, asking permission from Mom. I left with Kat and Lemon, feeling guilty and elated at the same time.

KAT KNEELED on the ground with a small rake and moved the sand around. "I think I found something, Sera, Lemon."

. . .

"WHAT IS IT?" Lemon asked.

"IT'S A MONEY CLIP, I THINK." She picked it up in her gloved hands for us to see.

"THAT'S NOT something a kid would have," I said.

"Exactly, Sera. It's an expensive one too. It's a good clue." (look up expensive money clips)

SHE PLACED it in a plastic bag. "Did you find anything, Sera? Lemon?"

I HAD FOUND nothing but shoe prints. Mostly tennis shoes or flat like sandals or flip-flops. I had taken photos of them. But was this an FBI-grade clue? Or as Damica and Kat had said, Nancy Drew makes mistakes too. I didn't want to make a mistake on my first FBI job. I found a really clear imprint of a tennis shoe and took a picture.

"HOW ABOUT A REPEATING SHOE IMPRINT?" I said. I held up my camera screen so Lemon and Kat could see.

. . .

"ARE you seeing that shoe print a lot?" Lemon asked.

"YES, it seems to be on top of all the other ones."

"AS IF THE person came later after the party was over?"

"MAYBE," I said. Not sure if my clue was a clue or just someone walking around the bonfire after everyone had left.

"LET ME SEE THAT," Lemon said, grabbing my camera. "That's an expensive brand. Not something a teen would have unless he were making $500 extra bucks a few times a week."

"Yes," Kat said. "That is a great clue, Sera! And since the prints are overtop of everyone else's, he's probably cleaning the scene after the party."

"SO, HE'S IN ON IT?" I asked.

"I THINK SO," Kat said.

. . .

"HEY WHAT HAPPENED to the two other guys that were hanging around with bandana-guy (Brennan)?"

"WE HAVEN'T BEEN able to locate them," Kat said. "They're in the wind, so to speak."

AFTER ANOTHER HOUR, we packed up our stuff and headed back to the beach house. The shoe print and money clip were the only things we had found. Someone had cleaned the scene really well.

BACK AT THE BEACH HOUSE, Lemon and Kat said their goodbyes and left. I went upstairs to rest. The adrenaline rush of the day had fizzled out. My arm ached. I needed a nap. As I snuggled under the covers, Mom approached the bedroom, holding a small tray with a pill bottle, a glass of water, and a plate of snacks.

THE NEXT THING I KNEW, Sam was shaking me. I woke up feeling disoriented and groggy. It was dark. His face was close to mine, making his nose large like a bad guy's.

"SERA, WAKE UP. ISABELLA IS MISSING."

· · ·

"WHAT?" I sat up quickly.

"YES, she said she's going to sleuth on her own."

"DO MOM AND DAD KNOW?"
   "Yes, they're on the beach looking for her."

"WHERE'S JOSIAH?"

"HE'S with Agent Jim Gains for something. I'm not sure what it is, but he hasn't returned yet."

"CALL KAT!" I yelled as I shoved my legs into some shorts.

"I'M HERE!" Josiah yelled from the bottom of the stairs. "I saw Mom and Dad on the beach. They filled me in."
   "What were you doing with Agent Gains?" I accused, my voice laced with bitterness. A pang of jealousy twisted inside me as they arranged to meet without inviting me.
   "What? Sera, that doesn't matter right now. We need to find Isabella."
   "Wait, where's Mandy?"

"Sorry to be the bearer of more bad news, but she's sitting downstairs waiting for her parents." Josiah said, patting me on the head and then handing me a pair of tennis shoes.

"Why?" I asked.

"Mom and Dad reached out to them and shared the news of you being shot. They don't want her in danger."

"Yeah, and she's not allowed to be your friend anymore," Sam added, twisting the knife of rejection, a close acquaintance of jealousy.

I slid a no-show sock on my foot and put a tennis shoe on. My thoughts were a swirling mess. Mandy is my best friend. She's Bess to my Nancy. How will I sleuth without her? She understands me like no one else. As I slid the shoe over my foot, another thought popped into my mind.

"Josiah, do you remember what kind of shoes bandana-guys friends were wearing?" I said.

"Shouldn't you go say goodbye to Mandy?" Josiah asked.

"Yes, I'm going to. But this is important. Look at the pictures on my camera." I grabbed my camera off the nightstand and held it out to him. "I'm going downstairs to tell Mandy goodbye."

Josiah took the camera. I tied my shoes and ran downstairs. Mandy's parents were there, grabbing her suitcase and heading out the door.

"Mandy," I said.

"I'm sorry Sera," she said. A tear rolled down her cheek and into her mouth.

"Let's go, Mandy," her father said.

"Sera, Mandy won't be seeing you anymore," her mom said.

"But she's my best friend," I shouted.

"You put her in danger. You're not a good influence," her dad said.

Tears streamed down Mandy's face as they forcefully pulled her away, her eyes filled with despair. I hit the floor with both knees and wept.

Josiah kneeled beside me and gave me a reassuring pat on the back.

"Is *sob* true? I'm bad?"

"NO, SERA IT'S NOT."

I LOST my best friend and my sister is missing. Could life get any worse? My presence seemed to bring chaos and discord to this once peaceful family.

There was a ping at the door.

"IT'S GEORGE," Sam yelled. "I'll get it."

I WAS STILL CURLED up in a little ball on the floor when George burst in yelling, "Guys, I think I found where they keep the girls before they ship them out."

"What?" Josiah said, standing and leaving me on the floor.

"Hey, what's going on?" George asked, directing his attention to me. "Is her arm hurting?"

"Isabella's missing and Mandy's parents just took her and told Sera she couldn't be around her anymore," Josiah said quickly. "Now, show us!"

Sam and Josiah were already running towards the back door. I stood shakily and said, "Wait for me, I'm coming too!"

Chapter 14

I was still mad at Josiah for meeting Agent Gains without me, but I stuffed the anger down. There were two priorities right now - finding Isabella and the girls they were getting ready to ship out.

Josiah, Sam, and I ran down the beach, following George. We passed Mom and Dad, who were questioning some people on the beach. Dad had his phone up. He must have been showing them a picture of Isabella. A tall, fit man wearing bright blue swimming trunks shook his head in the affirmative as we passed. Dad took off at a jog towards us.

"I've got something!" he said, waving his phone in the air.

We slowed to a jog as Mom and Dad joined us. That man saw Isabella at the hotel you were having the FBI meetings at.

"Call Agent Gains," Mom huffed.

"Which one?" Josiah said.

"Both," Dad said.

"Aren't we going the wrong way?" Sam asked. "The hotel is the other direction."

Dad stopped and put his hands on his knees. "I need to catch * my *breath. We need to split up."

"Yes, George has a lead," Josiah said. "He knows where they hold the girls until they ship out."

"That sounds like a job for the FBI," Mom said.

"No offense Mrs. Craven, but the FBI hasn't found my sister yet."

"Dad, Mom, I'll go with George. We won't go in until we have some agents with us." Josiah said.

Oh, the agony I was feeling. Josiah was going to scoop the FBI, find the girls, and solve the case. I wanted to go with him. But I wanted to find Isabella. I couldn't lose her. I had already lost Mandy forever.

Agent Jim Gains joined us on the beach, jogging up to us. He ran like Woody from Toy Story, his legs and arms flailing. Dad filled him in and we split up.

The guys were running down the beach with Agent Jim on the phone, arranging for a team to meet them at the site George had given him.

Mom and Dad were jogging the other way. Dad was on the phone with hotel management. I stood for what seemed like forever in the middle, watching both groups, wishing I could split myself in half.

Following Mom and Dad, I took one last look at Josiah, Sam, George, and Agent Jim. I smoldered inside. I was Nancy Drew. It was my duty to solve the case. Isabella had messed everything up. Josiah and Sam were going to get all the glory. They would probably become the world's youngest FBI agents instead of me.

Dad stopped and turned towards Mom and me. "The manager said Isabella isn't at the hotel and never has been."

"Why would a random stranger lie?" I asked.

"Maybe he was mistaken," Mom said.

We were one block from the hotel. "Why don't we check anyway?" I asked.

"Okay," Dad said. "We don't know where else to look anyway."

In the hotel lobby, I spotted Phylis' husband talking to the manager. "Let's ask Phylis' husband," I suggested.

"Great idea, Sera."

Damica intercepted us and said, "I simply wanted to inform you that we have a portion of our team out searching for Isabella. You were right to come here. This is exactly where I think she would come. This is where Sera came for the briefings."

"The manager said she hadn't been here." Dad explained.

Damica's eyes narrowed. "Oh, did he now?" She shook her head and her blonde curls flew around. Confusion spread across her face.

"Were you going to talk to the manager?" she asked.

"No, we were actually going to talk to the man who is talking to him. He's one of our neighbors who is on vacation with his wife and kids."

"Interesting," Damica said. "I hate to ask you this,

but could you record your conversation? And ask the manager the questions you asked him on the phone?"

"We need to find Isabella," Mom said.

"This will help. I promise. Trust me."

Yahoo, not only were we going to find Isabella, but I was going undercover right here in the hotel. Something wasn't right. That's what Damica thought, and I was going to find out what.

"I'll be in the conference room. I need to contact our computer hacker, Maryanne." And she strode quickly away.

Dad, Mom, and I approached the desk. "Hi," Dad said. "Remember us, this is my wife, Clare, and daughter, Sera. We really need your help. Our daughter, Isabella disappeared."

He held up the photo. Mom's phone was recording. The manager didn't even glance at the photo.

"As I told you on the phone, sir, I haven't seen her. She hasn't been here."

Phylis' husband looked and said, "No, I haven't seen her either."

A loud, shrill bark resounded in the lobby. I turned to see Lemon's dog, Rusty, running at break-neck speed.

"You can't have dogs in here," the manager yelled.

Lemon ran by us in pursuit of Rusty. She flashed a badge as she ran by.

The manager slipped out from behind the desk and took off in pursuit of Lemon and Rusty. Phylis' husband followed. Mom, Dad, and I stood there. Dumbfounded.

Damica came running out of the hallway next to the manager's desk and yelled. "Follow Lemon!"

So we did. Rusty ran to the entrance to the stairwell and barked. Lemon opened it and followed the dog. Dad, Mom, and I took off after them. Damica was in front of dad, but he passed her. We ran down, sounding like a herd of elephants into the deep bowels of the hotel. We exited into a dark, damp room, full of pipes hissing, laundry carts, and a low ceiling.

Rusty kept running. We snaked around the labyrinth of the basement until Rusty stopped in front of a locked metal door. The hotel manager stood in front of the door and said, "That's far enough." He pulled out a gun.

"You've gone too far. Put that gun away." Phylis' husband said, his face drained of all color.

"That's funny," he said, waving the gun around. "Does your wife have knowledge of your activities?" Does she know you, traffic girls, to afford all of this?" He waved his arm around for emphasis.

I stood behind dad, thinking. Struggling to understand everything.

"Don't say anything else," Phylis's husband said. "You're ruining everything."

"You know what else is hilarious. We have an FBI task force to take down human trafficking right here in the hotel and they don't have a clue." He pointed to the door. "We've been doing this right under their noses. The fake burglaries were a great red herring.

We could see who had girls the right age and how should I say, looks?"

"Stop it," Phylis' husband said.

"No need. These people are never going to tell. And this hotel provided the right clientele."

In the movies, this was the part where everyone promised they wouldn't tell. Then they got shot. In Nancy Drew's books, this is when she did something heroic or someone did. Who was that going to be? Dad had a firm grip on me. It would not be me. He wouldn't let me get shot again. Mom was behind me, sandwiching me in.

"You're right, Damica said, "You outsmarted us. Since you're going to kill us anyway, why don't you fill us in on how this operation works. It's obviously well thought out and executed."

The bitter taste of dread filled my mouth as I contemplated the gruesome fate that awaited us.

"You know what's going on right now? You have your team raiding an empty building. All the girls have been right here under your nose the whole time." He laughed.

"Rusty," Lemon whispered. Rusty sprang into action, bit the manager's hand, and the gun clattered to the ground. Damica kicked the gun under some pipes while the manager yelled "What the cuss, you cuss!"

"Open the door!" Goosebumps formed on my skin as a shiver ran down my spine at the sound of the voice. Kat stepped out, pointing a gun. Shadowy agents, all dressed in black and pointing guns at the manager, followed her. Rusty wagged his tail and retreated to Lemon's side.

Phylis' husband swiftly snatched the jingling keys from the manager's jacket pocket and smoothly inserted one into the lock. With a creak, the heavy gray metal door swung open. And behind it was the most beautiful sight I had ever seen. Isabella.

"I did it!" she said, spreading her arms out wide. I sluiced, followed the clues, and found the girls. "I knew that manager was bad. I mentioned to him that I was an orphan and you all decided to abandon me."

Damica, Kat, Lemon, and some other members of the task force entered the room and freed the five other girls, who were all weeping with relief.

Dad, Mom, and I were hugging Isabella. "I knew you would find me. I was the bait. Did I do a good job?" Isabella was asking.

Out of the corner of my eye, I saw George enter the room, followed by Josiah and Sam, who joined us in squeezing Isabella.

"Emily!" George yelled. He quickly approached a disheveled, haunted-looking teen and lifted her in his arms.

Chapter 15

I didn't solve the case. But at least I witnessed the case being solved. I breathed a sigh of relief, knowing Isabella was out of harm's way. Emily, George's sister, is alive.Five other teens, disheveled and crying, exited the basement.

I could hear the low murmur of conversation as the agents explained the situation to the paramedics. The agents handcuffed the hotel manager and Phyllis' husband, and led them away for questioning.

"How did you know?" I asked Kat.

"Why do you think we chose this hotel?" she chuckled.

"Oh," I said.

"Hotels are often hubs for human trafficking," she added. There appeared to be an extremely high rate of vacationers in this area, and the "Parties" were held close to this hotel. It simply made sense."

"Plus the burglaries. Those were scouting expeditions. The stolen items ranged from peculiar trinkets to valuable jewels, leaving investigators perplexed. At one house it was jewelry. The next it was credit cards. We worked with the local police on that," Damica added.

"Yes, it turns out that the targeting focused on families. Especially families with girls of a certain age."

"But someone robbed Phyllis," I said.

"Think about it, Sera." Kat chuckled again.

"Her husband did it!" I said.

"You got it!" Kat said.

"That jewelry didn't matter to him because he hid it. Remember only Phyllis displayed an emotional reaction to the robbery," Lemon added.

"Sera, let's go," Dad said, patting me on the shoulder. "Let's let the task force finish their work."

"Thanks for all your help, Ben. So sorry about Isabella." Kat said.

"I think we need to get her home," Mom said.

Honestly, Mom and Dad looked more haggard than Isabella. She glowed. She "sluiced" which made her feel like part of the team and the family.

We left the hotel - the whole family - minus Mandy and strolled back to the beach house. It was over. Case solved. No more FBI. No more task force. Nothing but a typical, uneventful vacation.

At that precise moment, Agent Jim caught up with us.

"Hey, Craven family. We are going to have a celebratory dinner. Maryanne's idea. She's our computer gal. Anyway, she asked me to invite you because she's busy looking at all the files she gathered on the ring."

"Sure," Dad said. "We have something to celebrate, don't we?" He picked up Isabella and twirled her around.

"Okay, great. You'll meet Maryanne later. It's going to be quite the party. I'll text you the details."

My mood lifted, as did all those of the family. It made sense to celebrate. All things had lost their excitement and freshness even though all things had been resolved and Isabella had escaped trafficking.

Weird how life works. Something really good happens and instead of being happy, we are sad instead. I remember when I was first adopted; I felt that way. I was happy in the larger sense. I obtained what I always wanted, but I was still filled with sadness. Feeling sorrowful for leaving the people I had left behind.

Mom helped me. She opened up about her past and the challenges she encountered following her departure from the group home after being adopted. We both had something good, something we had always wanted. And the truth? I became accustomed to the constant chaos in the orphanage.

Does struggle become normal? And at that moment when joy and peace appear, what's the word Mom used? Anti-climatic. Or boring. Isabella found it harder to adjust to her new normal compared to me. She liked the chaos. She craved it. When it wasn't present, she created it. This was another example. I hoped Mom and Dad didn't take her back to the therapist.

"The therapist didn't know anything about trauma," I had overheard Mom say to dad. "She offers Isabella rewards. Rewards don't work."

"Squirt, you seem lost in thought," Josiah said, ruffling my hair.

"It's over, right?" I said, kicking the sand with my sandal.

"Yep, it's over," he said, grinning.

"The good guys won, Sera," Sam added. "Smile."

"That's exactly the point." We should be celebrating, right? But everyone looks glum and serious." I said.

"Sera, you're right," Mom said. "Let's have our own celebration before the task force one."

"What can we do?" I asked.

"Let's take a picnic down to the beach. Let's play in the sand and the water. That's what we are here for, right? Vacation." Mom said.

Isabella, Sam, and I said, "Yeah!" and took off running to the house to change.

Mom packed a cooler and picnic basket while we all changed into our bathing suits and grabbed our beach towels. We all helped carry stuff down to the beach. It was the best afternoon ever. We played in the waves. Ate lots of food. Laughed. Built sandcastles. Buried each other.

Later, we showered and changed for the party. Maryanne had sent us all outfits to wear. Isabella, Mom, and I had sundresses and sandals. The boys had dressy shorts, button-downs, and flip-flops. It was nice of her to send them, but more important than that, I was glad it wasn't super dressy. And the sundresses were in Nancy Drew style. So I was happy.

We met in the living room. Dad read the text with the directions. We were going to a beach bonfire! There were going to be fireworks. Best day ever! Maybe we'd stumble on another mystery to solve soon, but for now I was happy we'd solve The Case of The Missing Teen (And Isabella).

WHAT TO READ NEXT:
The Case Of The Missing Skeleton

Acknowledgments

Thanks to my husband for always supporting me and spending countless hours reading my manuscripts!

Stay in Touch

Hi! Building a relationship with my readers is super important to me. If I could, I'd sit down and have a cup of coffee with you. Since I can't do that, I'd love to keep you in the loop.

Hop on over to kathleenguireauthor.com to sign up to follow me by email. I'll keep you updated on new releases.

You can also email me - Kathleenguire@gmail.com

Last but not least -

Please leave a review. I count on readers like you!

Blessings,

Kathleen Guire

Notes

About the Author

Kathleen Guire is the mother of seven, four through adoption, former National Parent of the Year, author, teacher, and speaker. She loves connecting with readers through her website (Kathleenguireauthor.com).

For more information,
about Kathleen, check out her website and follow her on social media!

www.kathleenguireauthor.com
kathleenguire@gmail.com

Also by Kathleen Guire

What to read next

The Case Of The Missing Skeleton

Made in the USA
Columbia, SC
20 November 2024

46753267R00070